This book belongs to:

. . . . . . . . . . . . . . . . . . . . . .

First published in the UK in 2015 by HarperCollins *Children's Books*,
a division of HarperCollins Publishers Ltd, 1 London Bridge Street, London, SE1 9GF.
This edition published by HarperCollins *Children's Books* in 2019.
HarperCollins*Publishers* Macken House, 39/40 Mayor Street Upper  Dublin 1, D01 C9W8, Ireland

5 7 9 10 8 6

ISBN: 978-0-00-797709-3

Based on the script by Lead Writers: Ted Dewan and Philip Bergkvist and Team Writers: Lucy Murphy and Mikael Shields.

Adapted from the original books by Ted Dewan and using images created by Acamar Films, Brown Bag Films and Tandem Ltd.

Edited by Stella Gurney.

Designed by Anna Lubecka.

# Bing™

# Hide and Seek

HarperCollins *Children's Books*

Round the corner,
not far away,
Bing wants to
be 'it' today!

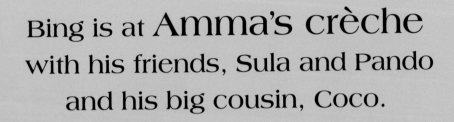

Bing is at **Amma's crèche**
with his friends, Sula and Pando
and his big cousin, Coco.

They decide to play
hide and seek.

"Can I be
'it' first?"
yells Coco.

"I want to
be 'it' too!"
says Bing.

"Choo choo,"
calls Sula.
"I need to do
a pee-pee."

"No problem,"
says Amma. "Let's
stop the game for
the toilet train!"

"I don't **need** to do the
**toilet train**," says Bing.

"Ok Bing,
**that's fine**,"
says Amma.

"All aboard the toilet train," says Amma.

"Stop the train for me,
I need to do a wee...!

...Choo choo choo choo,
choo choo choo choo wee wee...!"

Coco is 'it' first. She covers her eyes and starts counting. Everyone runs to hide.

Bing looks around for somewhere to hide.

"Bing!" whispers Flop. "What about hiding here, in the **lost and found basket?**"

Bing runs towards
the basket. But, oh no
– now he does need a wee!

"...four...
five...
six..."

counts Coco.

No time! Bing dashes
over towards the lost
and found basket
and dives in.

# "...seven..."

Coco is still counting.

"Oh, choo choo!" groans Bing.

Flop whispers into the basket, "Bing – if you need to go, we can stop the game."

"No!" Bing whispers, "I can't! Coco will see me and I'll be finded. I want to be 'iiiitt'!"

"Are you sure you can hold it?"
asks Flop. Bing nods.

"...eight...

nine...

ten!

Ready or
not, here
I come!"
shouts Coco.

She starts searching
the room.

Coco keeps searching.

"Nggggttt!"

squirms Bing, trying to hold his wee in.

Coco **hears**. She **stops**. She **creeps** over towards the lost and found basket.

Bing **is** the last to be found. Coco lifts
the lid of the basket and out **pops** Bing!

"Yay! I'm 'IT'!"
shouts Bing.

Sula runs up to give him a **big hug**.
"Let's play again!" she laughs.

"Bing needs to catch the
**toilet train** first," says Flop.

"Sorry, Amma. I tried to hold it in," sniffs Bing.

"Oh you tried to hold it in and you couldn't, that's ok, Bing," says Amma.

"**Hands up** everybody if you couldn't hold your **pee-pee** sometime?" Amma asks the others.

"Me!" shouts Pando.

"And me!" says Sula.

"Not since I was **oldish**," whispers Coco.

"Right," says Amma. "So Bing, what will you do next time you need to go pee-pee?"

"Choo choo!" says Bing.

"Now then, let's find you some dry pants," says Amma.

"One...
two...
three..."

Now Bing's changed
his pants and it's his
turn to be 'it'.

Good for you, Bing Bunny!

**Hi!** I was **hiding** so I didn't do the **toilet train** when everybody else did.

And Coco **finded** me last so I was 'it'.

But then I went **pee-pee** in my dungarees and that wasn't very nice.

But Amma cleaned it up and found me **dry** pants.

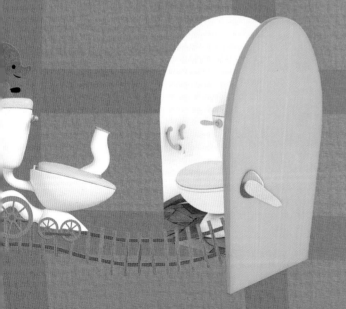

You need to pee-pee **before** you play... or **stop** the game and do it.

# Catching the toilet train...

## it's a Bing thing.